A Day in the Life of a...

Dentist

Carol Watson

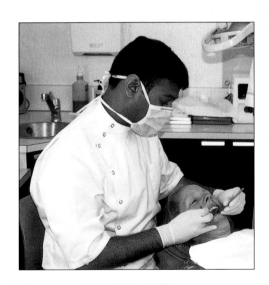

W

FRANKLIN WATTS

LONDON•SYDNEY

Ravi is a dentist. He starts work
at 8 am in the dental practice
which he shares with his
partner, Ailsa.

First Ravi changes
into his gown.
Then he asks Maureen,
the receptionist, about
the patients who are
booked in for that day.

His first appointment is with Sarah.
She is a new patient so she has to
write down the name of her doctor,
any illnesses she has had and
if she is taking any medicines.

In his surgery Ravi and the dental nurse prepare for work. The nurse takes the equipment out of the sterilizer.

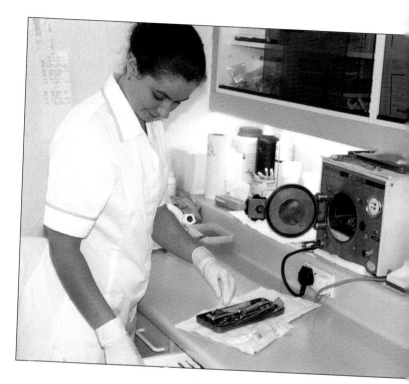

Ravi puts on his mask and gloves. These help to stop germs spreading.

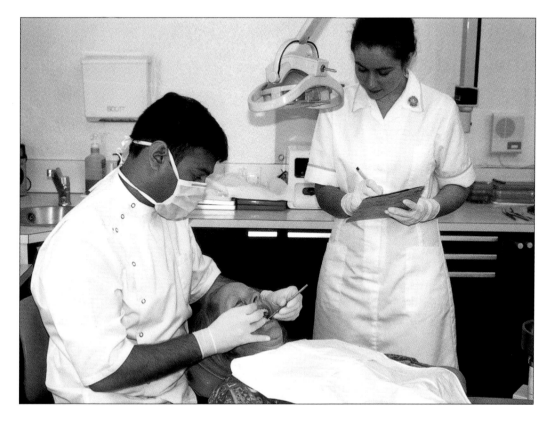

"Right, Sarah, now I'm going to have a good look at your teeth," says Ravi. Sarah lies back in the dentist's chair.

The nurse writes down the information about the teeth on a record card.

Next Ravi uses a machine to take
X-ray pictures of Sarah's jaw. These
will help to show Ravi if there is
anything wrong inside Sarah's mouth.

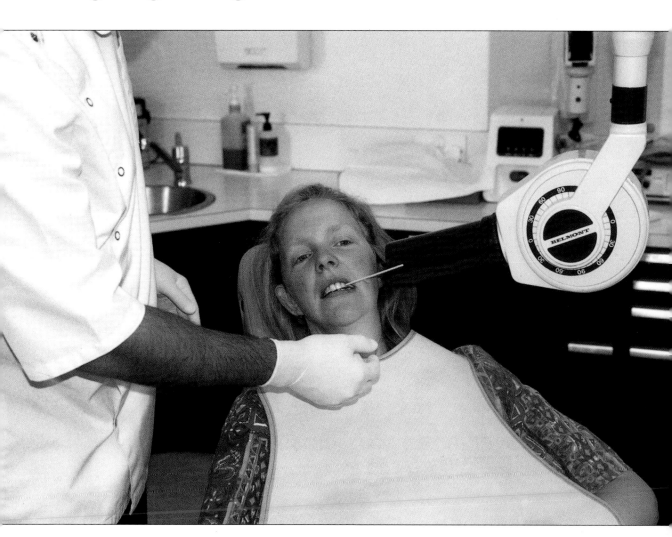

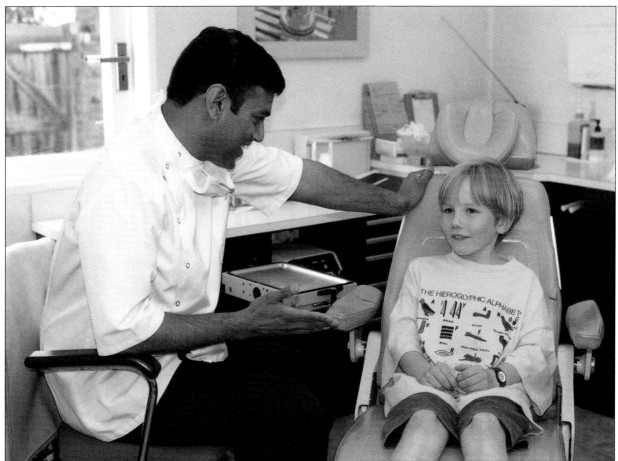

Charlie is the next patient. He has
come for a check-up. Ravi changes
his gloves and looks closely at
all of Charlie's teeth.

"Will you chew this blue tablet for me?" Ravi asks Charlie. "Then lick your teeth with your tongue."

"The blue bits on your teeth show where you have plaque and need to clean your teeth more carefully," explains Ravi. He shows Charlie how he should clean his teeth.

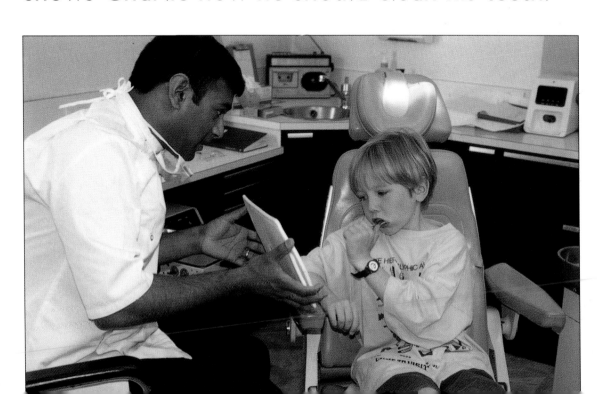

Then Ravi uses a machine to give Charlie's teeth a clean and a polish.

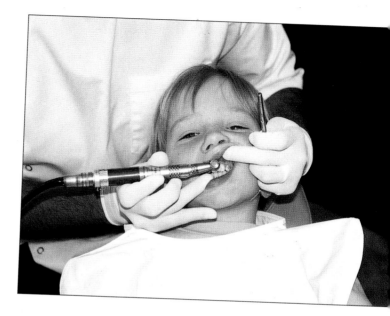

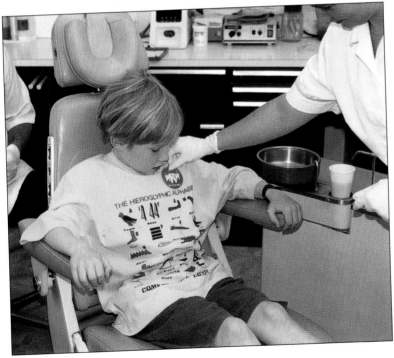

"All finished now," he says, and the nurse gives Charlie a sticker.

In the surgery next door, Ailsa is looking at Claudia's teeth. "One tooth has a hole in it," she tells Claudia. "I'll have to give you a filling."

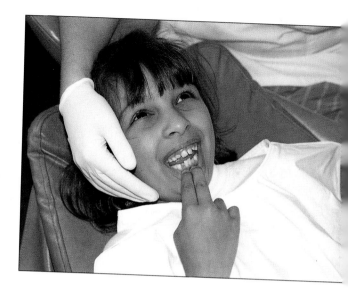

"These spectacles will stop any bits going into your eyes while I work," says Ailsa.

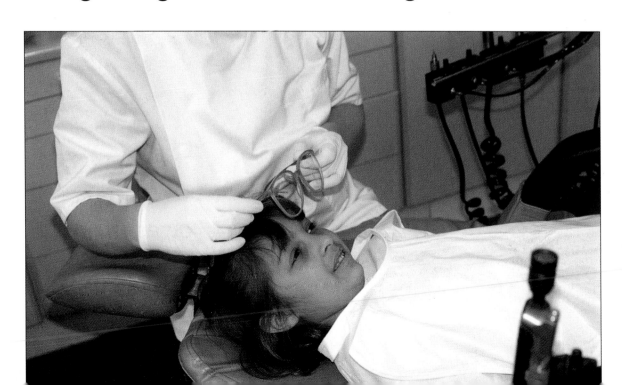

Ailsa freezes Claudia's gum so the drill won't hurt. The nurse stirs the mixture that makes the filling.

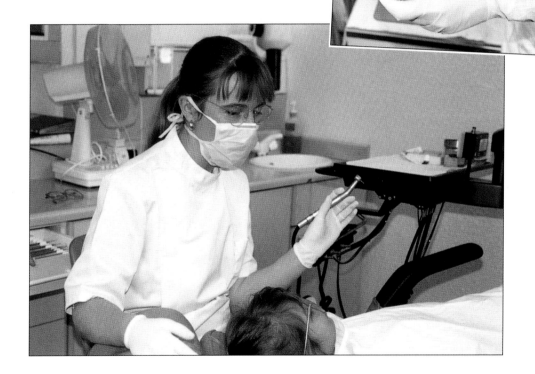

"That's it, Claudia," says Ailsa. "I'll just put in the filling and you'll be ready to go."

12

Claudia's sister, Clara, has an appointment with Ravi. He lifts her into the chair and the nurse puts on a white bib to protect Clara's clothes.

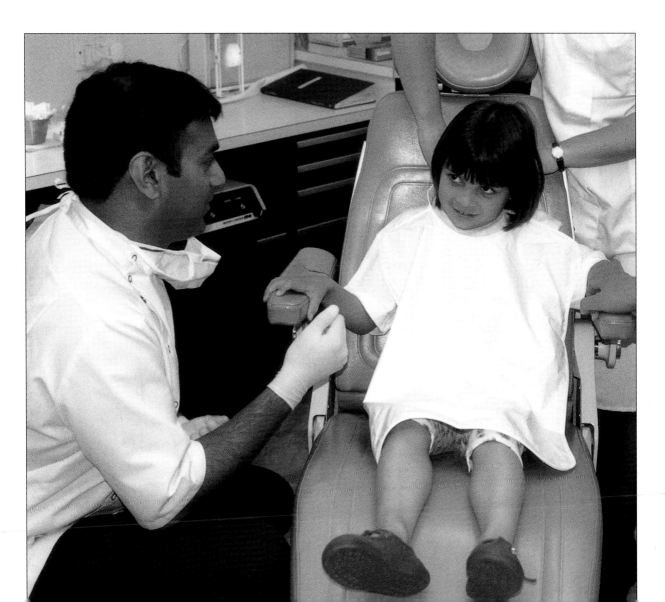

Before Ravi starts to treat Clara the receptionist interrupts. "Emergency patient, Ravi!" she tells him. A boy and his mother rush in.

"His front tooth has been knocked out!" says the boy's mother. "I've put it in milk to protect it."

It is important to get the tooth back into Ojay's gum as soon as possible. Ravi works quickly to put it in place.

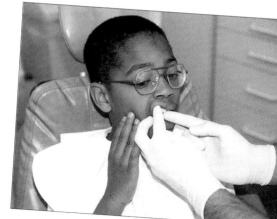

"He'll need to come back tomorrow for more treatment," Ravi tells the boy's mother.

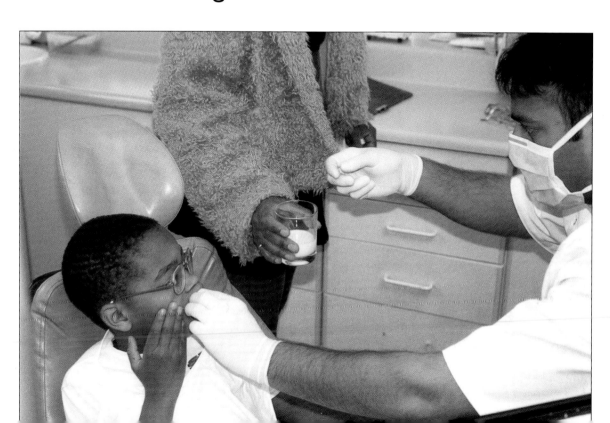

After a morning's hard work, Ravi
and Ailsa take a break for lunch.
"Poor Ojay," says Ravi. "But I think
we saved his tooth just in time."

Next the dentist makes a home visit. He packs his portable drill, fresh gloves and the other equipment he will need.

Mrs Potter cannot walk very well so it takes a long time for her to answer the door.

Ravi has come to fit a new set of dentures. He prepares the teeth and fits them into Mrs Potter's mouth.

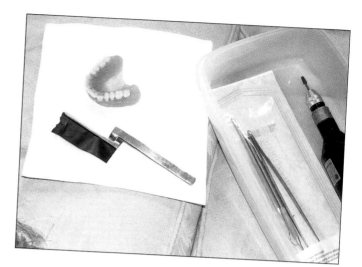

"Do those feel comfortable now?" he asks.

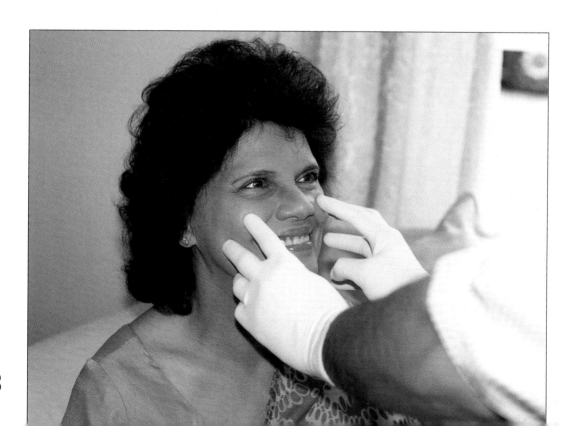

The dentist returns to the surgery. He has other patients to see before the end of the day.

When everyone has gone Ravi and Ailsa lock up. It's time to go home.

19

Plaque spotting

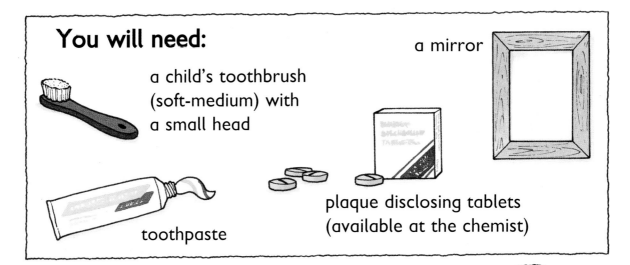

You will need:

a child's toothbrush
(soft-medium) with
a small head

toothpaste

plaque disclosing tablets
(available at the chemist)

a mirror

1. Brush your teeth with
toothpaste as usual.

2. Take a disclosing tablet and
chew it carefully (do not swallow
the tablet). Use your tongue
to spread the colour across
your teeth.

3. Look in the mirror at your teeth. The colour sticks to the parts of your teeth where there is still **plaque**. Look carefully to see where this is.

Plaque is a soft layer which forms on a tooth. It is full of bacteria which may cause tooth decay.

4. Now clean your teeth again. Gently scrub up and down but don't press too hard. Make sure you clean the areas that have plaque.

Always remember to clean thoroughly the areas that showed they had plaque.

How you can help your dentist look after your teeth

1. Always clean your teeth at least twice a day with a fluoride toothpaste.

2. Avoid eating sweets, chocolates and fizzy drinks between meals.

3. Eat an apple, raw carrot or cheese as a snack instead.

4. Change your toothbrush as soon as it becomes worn.

5. Have a dental check-up at least once a year.

6. **In case of accident** – if you lose a big front tooth try to put it back in position. If this is too difficult, put it in milk or inside your cheek immediately. Then go to a dentist as soon as possible.

Facts about dentists

There are different kinds of dentist. Ravi works in General Practice. His patients are all ages and come to him because he has been recommended to them by others. In order to do his job, Ravi had to study for five years at university or dental school and then do a year's further training before starting to work on his own. A dentist also has to be prepared to work with all kinds of people, and be able to calm down worried patients.

Other kinds of dentists work in hospitals, industry, in the armed forces and in the Community Dental Service (with the handicapped, elderly and children). Some teach in universities or do research.

Other people who work in dentistry are:
hygienists – they clean people's teeth and teach them how to look after their teeth and gums.
dental surgery assistants – qualified dental nurses who prepare the surgery, keep the dental records and help care for the patients.
dental technicians – they make the dentures and other things that dentists use to help people's teeth.

Index

© 1997 Franklin Watts

Franklin Watts
96 Leonard Street
London
EC2A 4XD

Franklin Watts Australia
14 Mars Road
Lane Cove
NSW 2066

ISBN: 0 7496 2616 X (hb)
  0 7496 3620 3 (pb)

Dewey Decimal Classification
Number: 617.6

10 9 8 7 6 5

A CIP catalogue record for
this book is available from the
British Library.

Printed in Malaysia

Editor: Sarah Ridley
Designer: Kirstie Billingham
Photographer: Harry Cory-Wright
Illustrations: Kim Woolley

With thanks to: Ailsa and Ravi
de Silva, Maureen Glanville,
Sheena Hales, Sarah Shehadi,
Charlie Wethered, Claudia and
Clara Bhugrah-Shmid, Ojay, Daniel
and Jennifer Morgan.